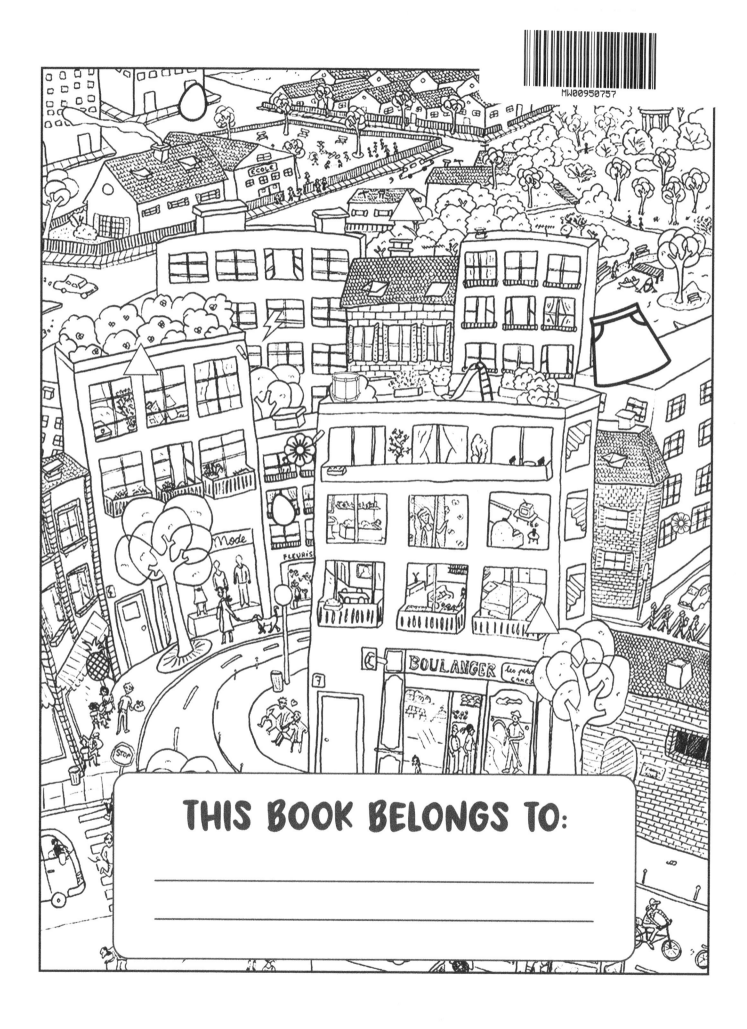

THIS BOOK BELONGS TO:

_____

_____

MW00950757

TEST YOUR COLORS HERE

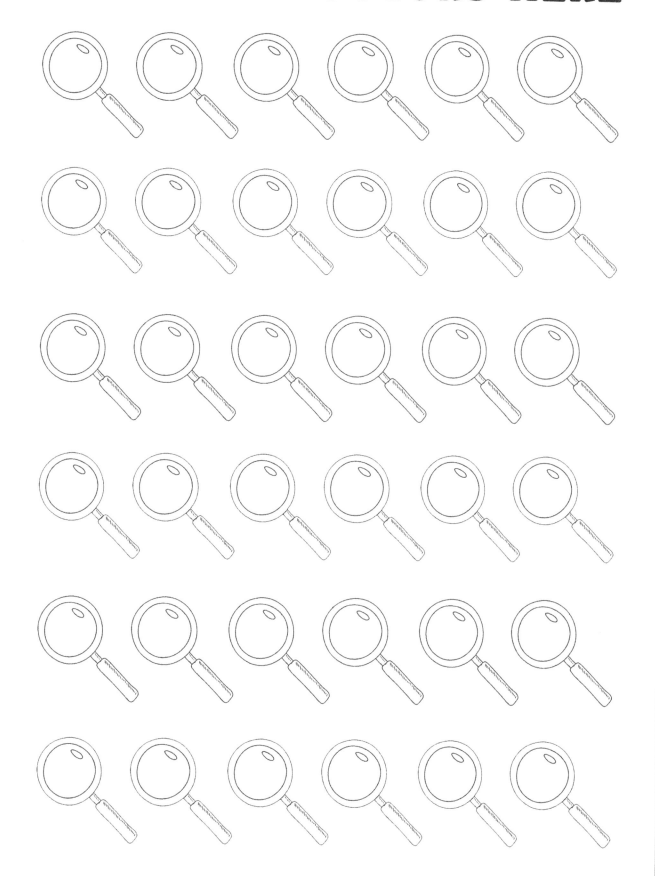

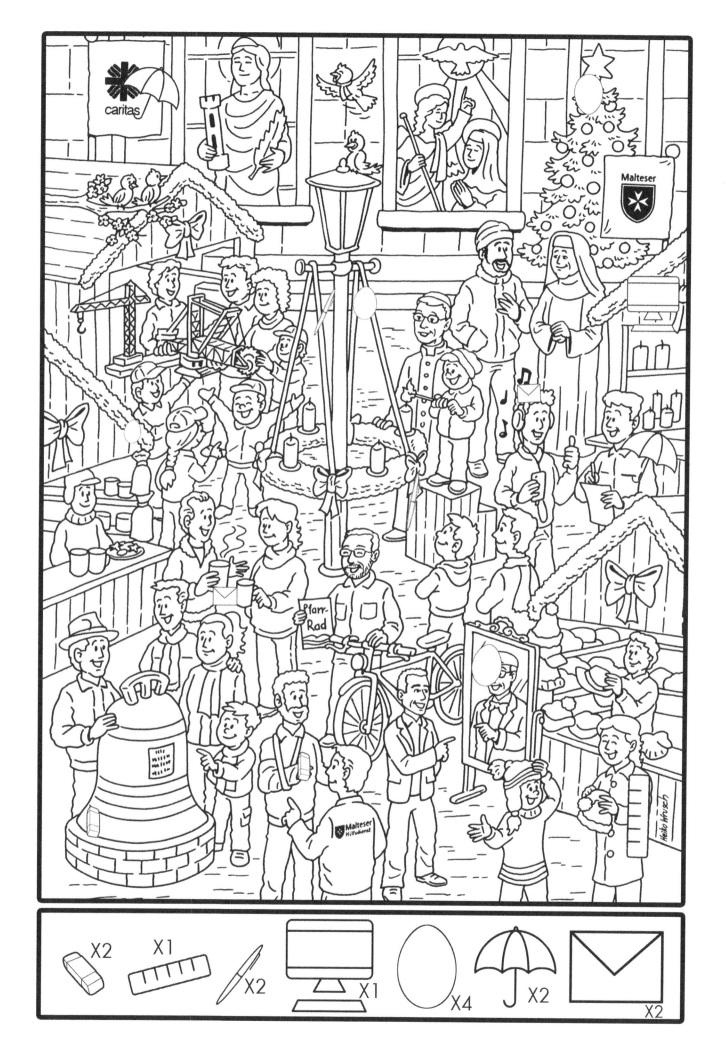

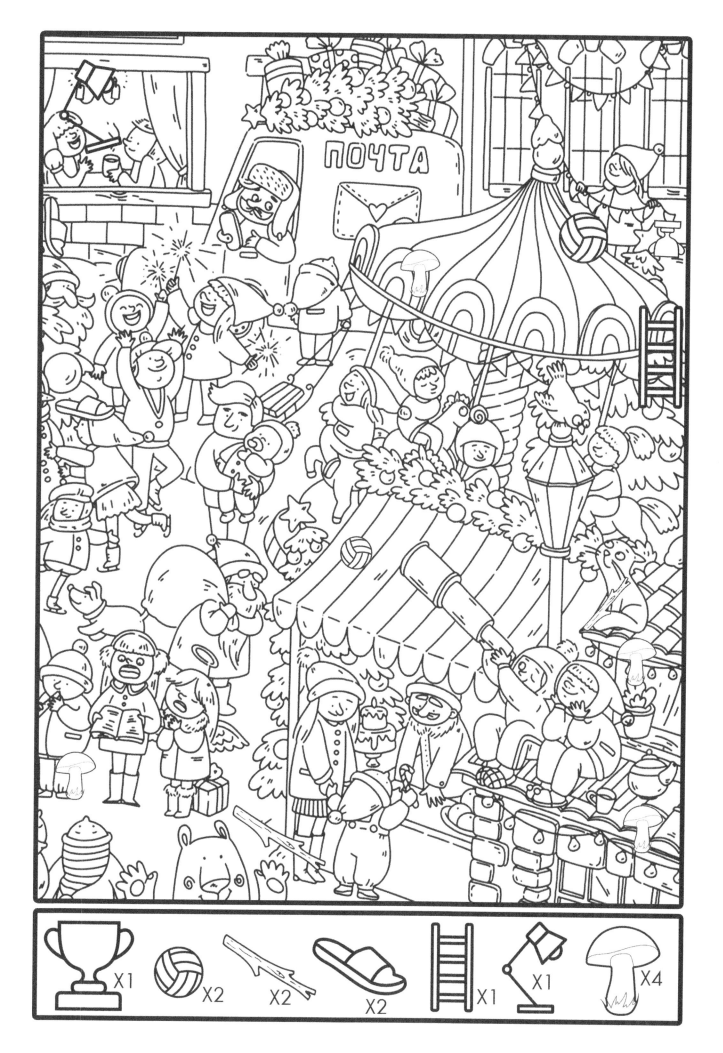

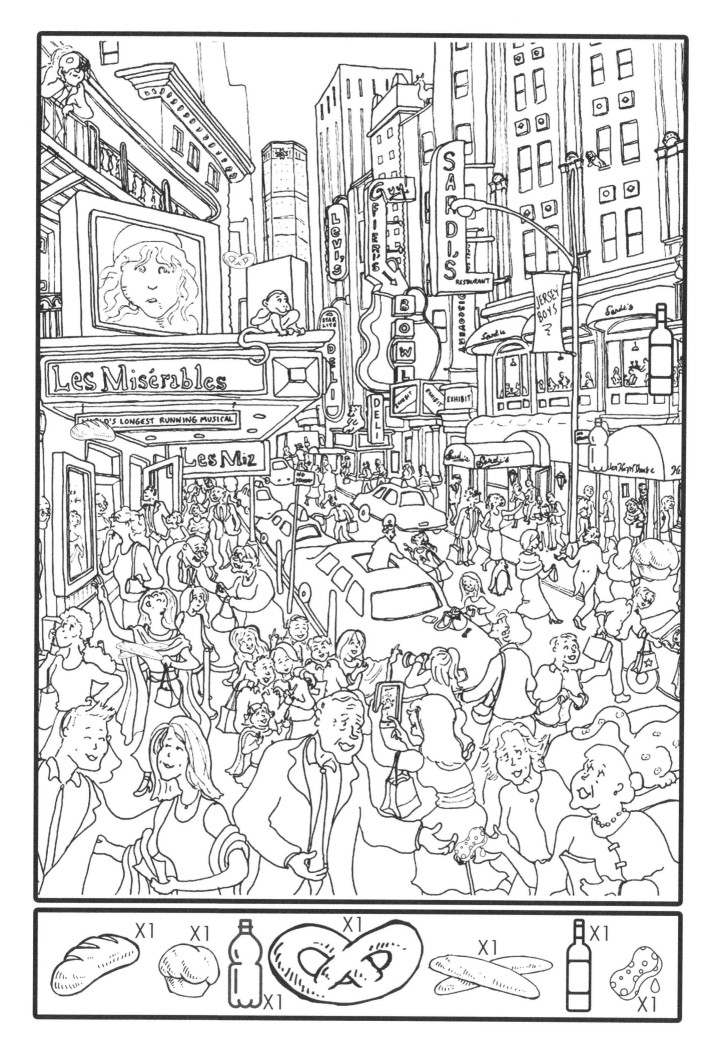

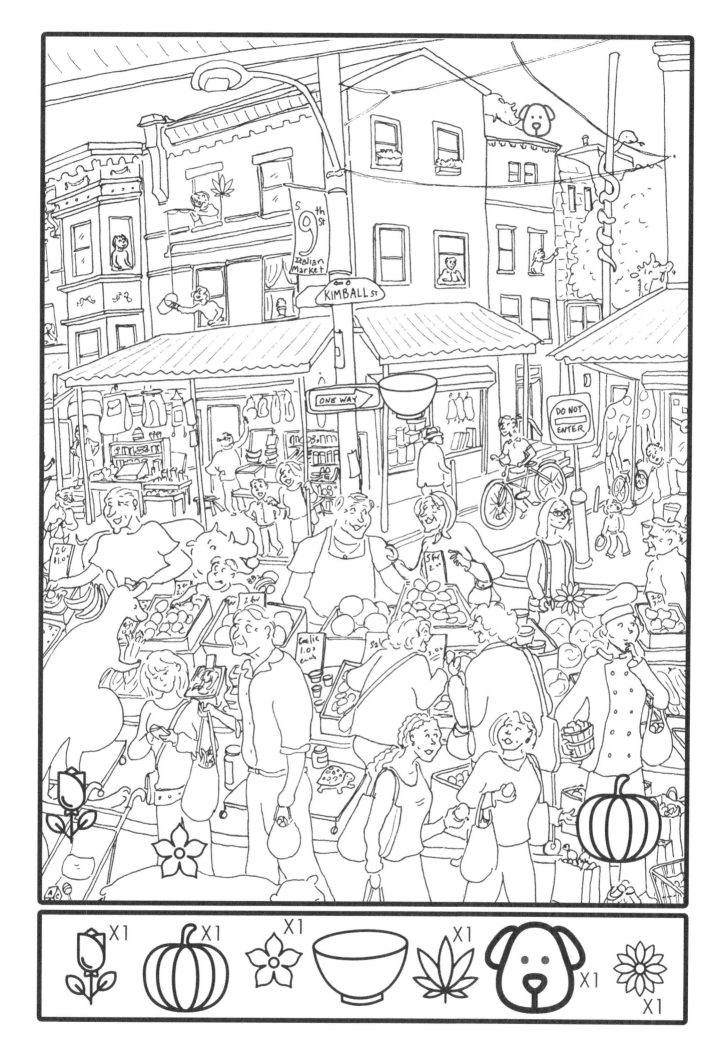

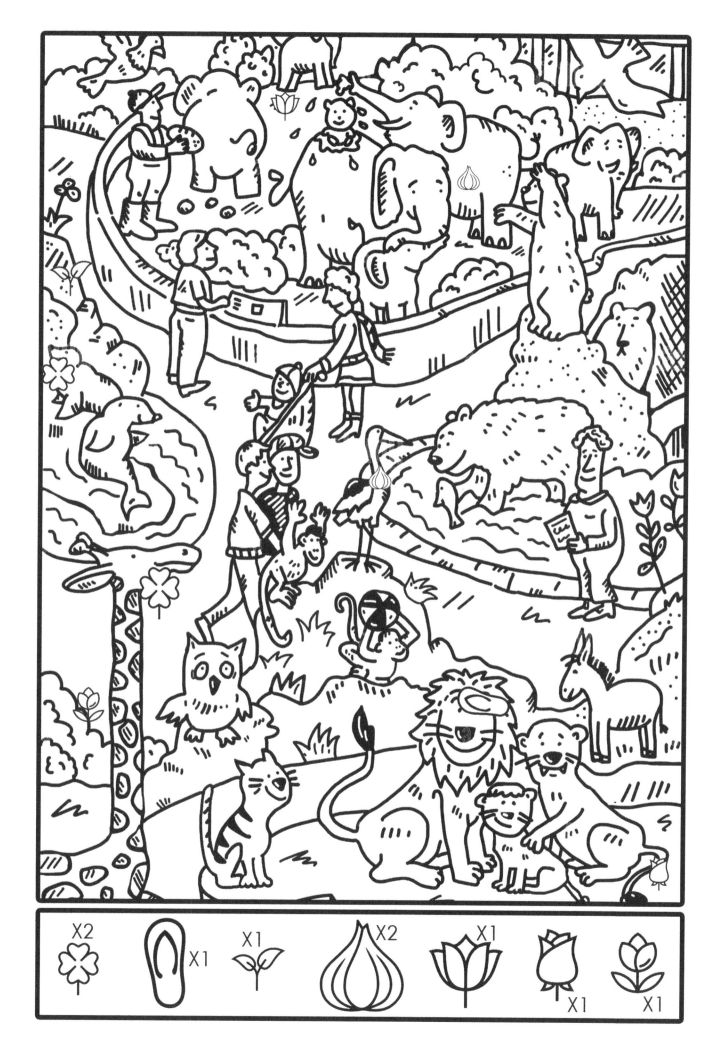

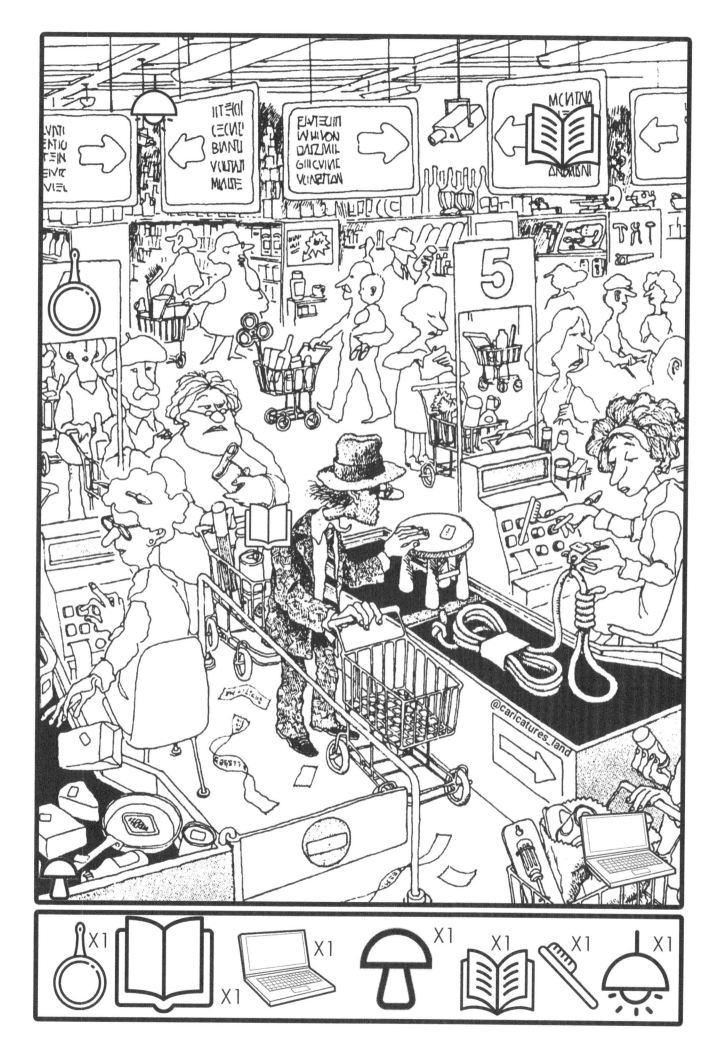

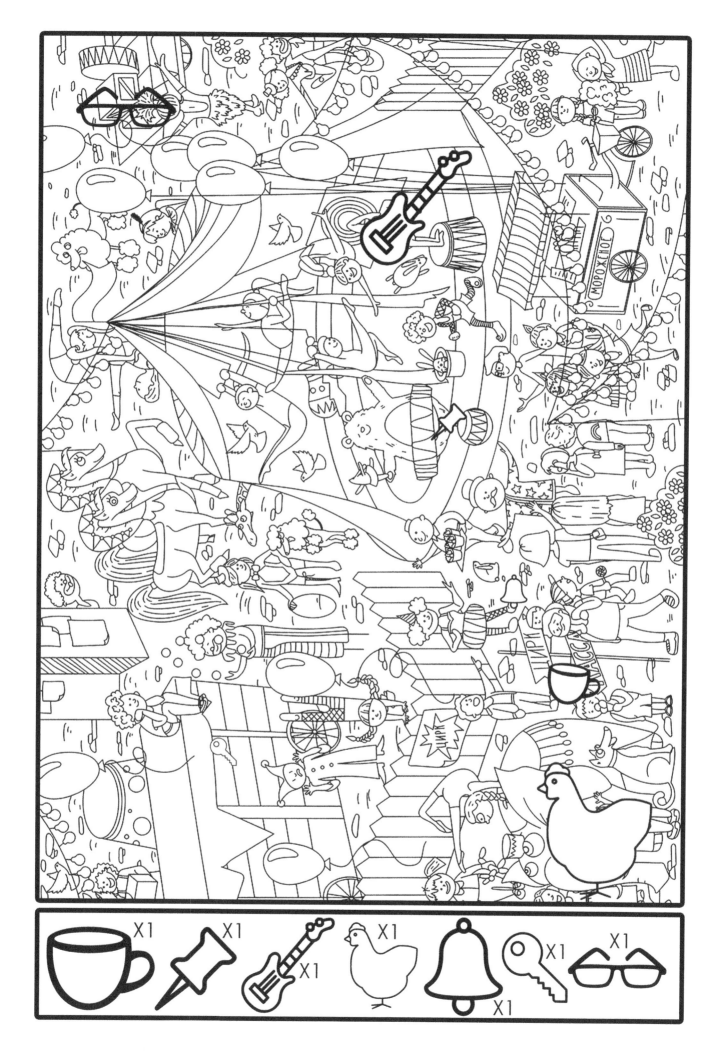

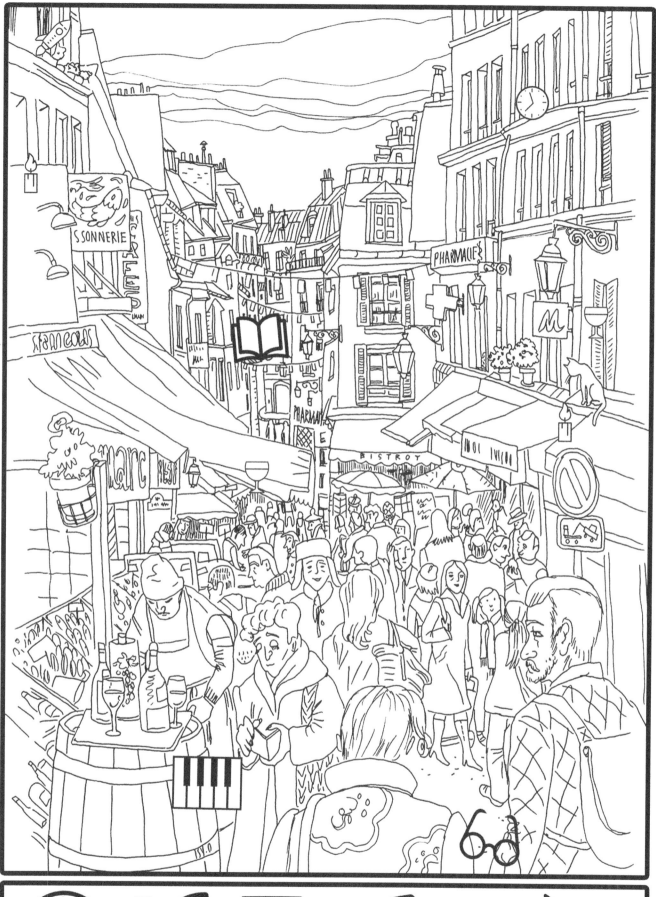
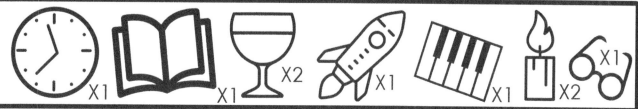

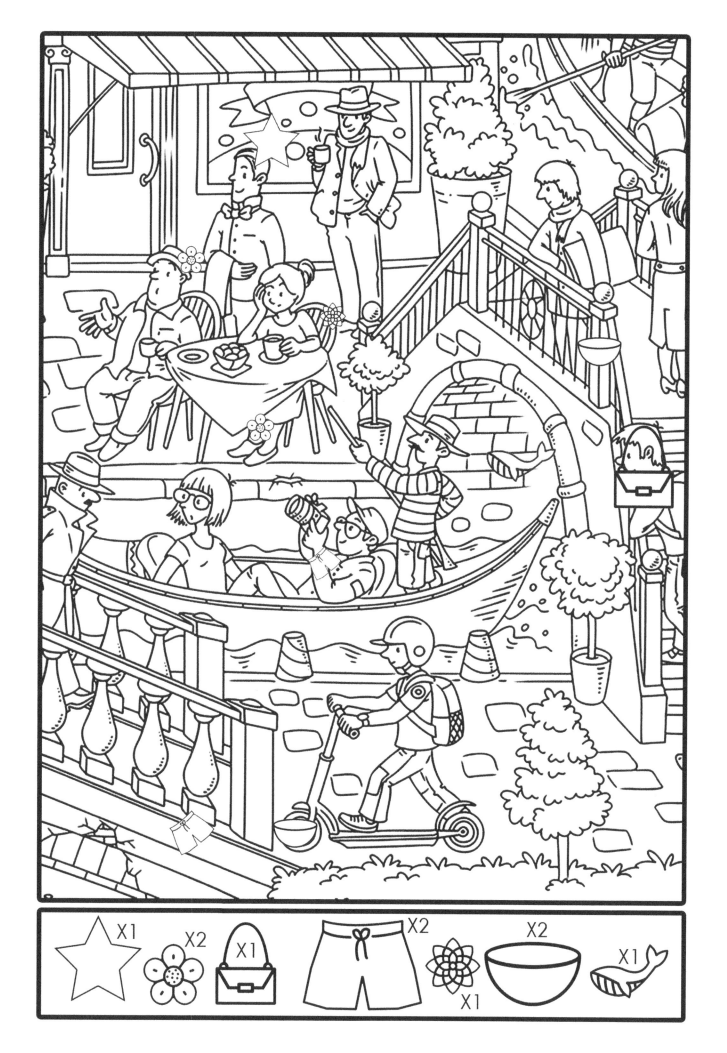

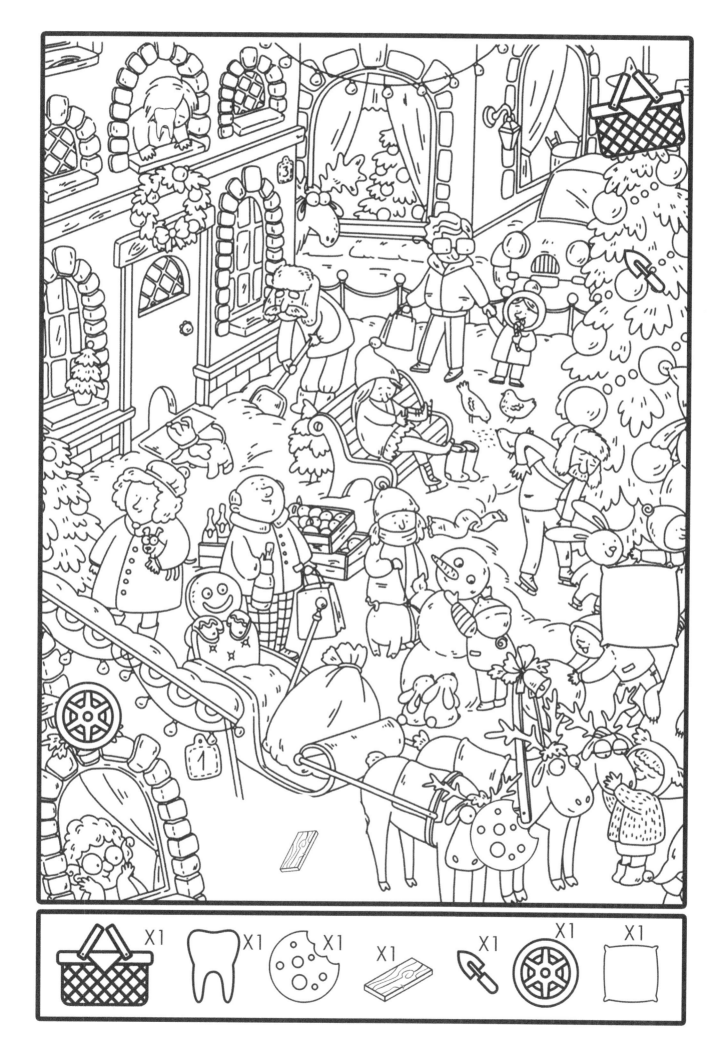

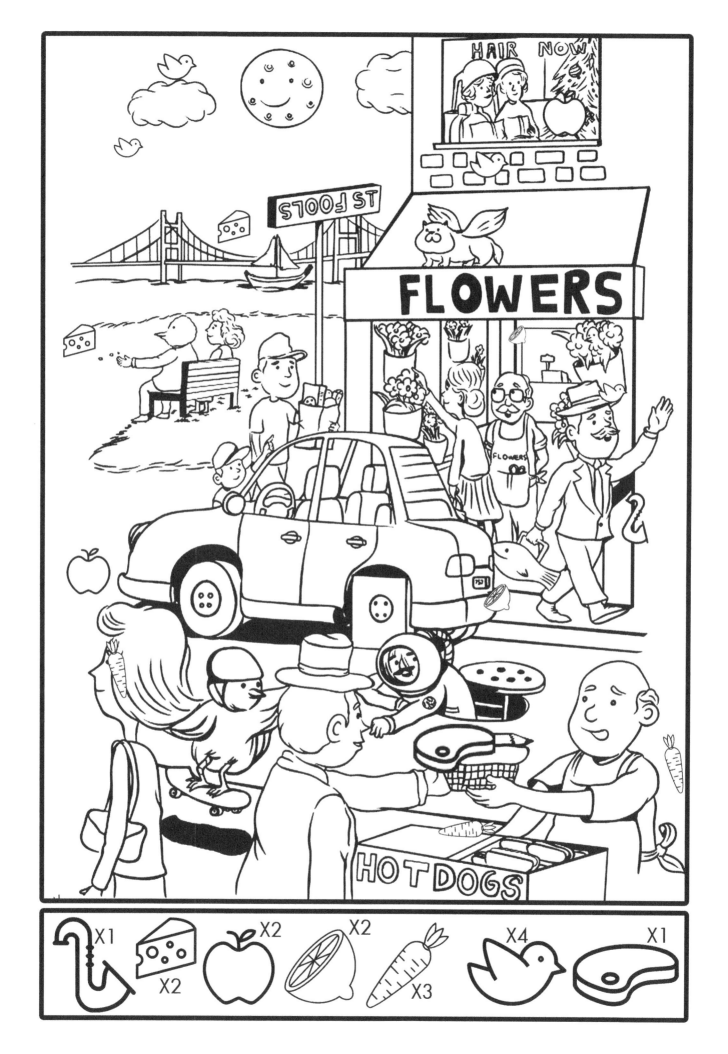

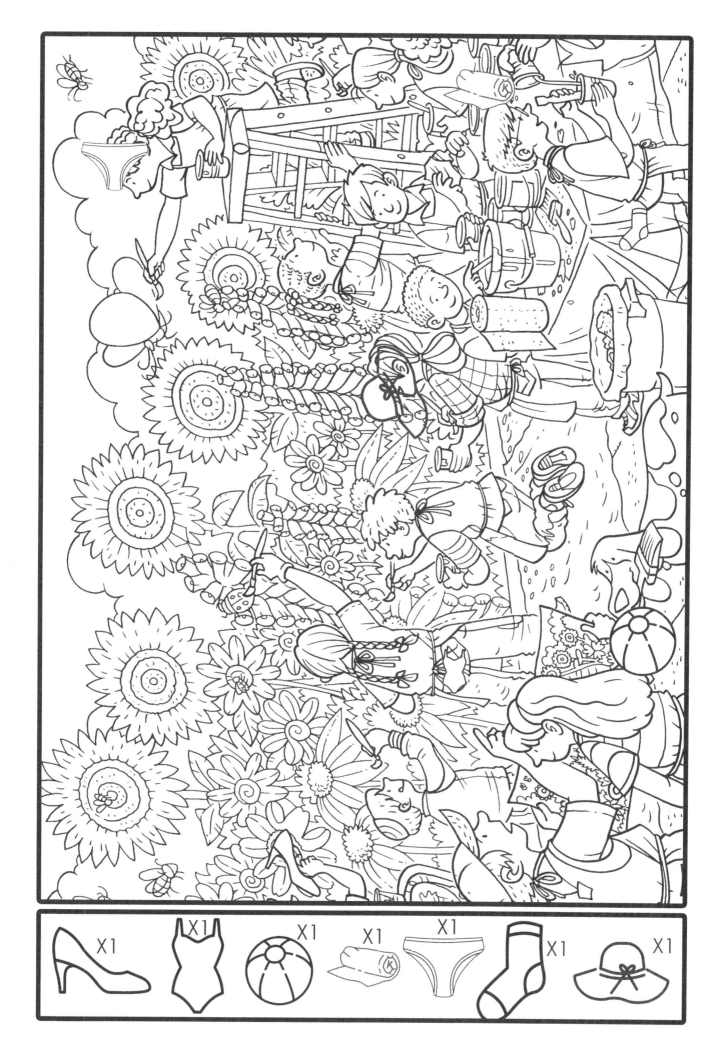

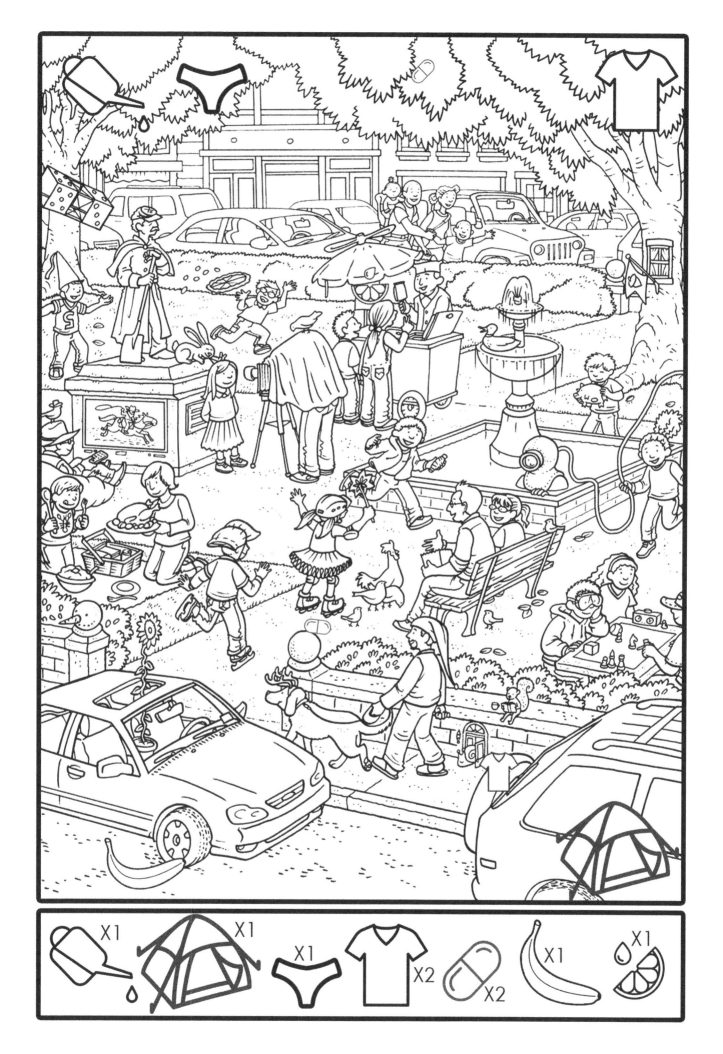

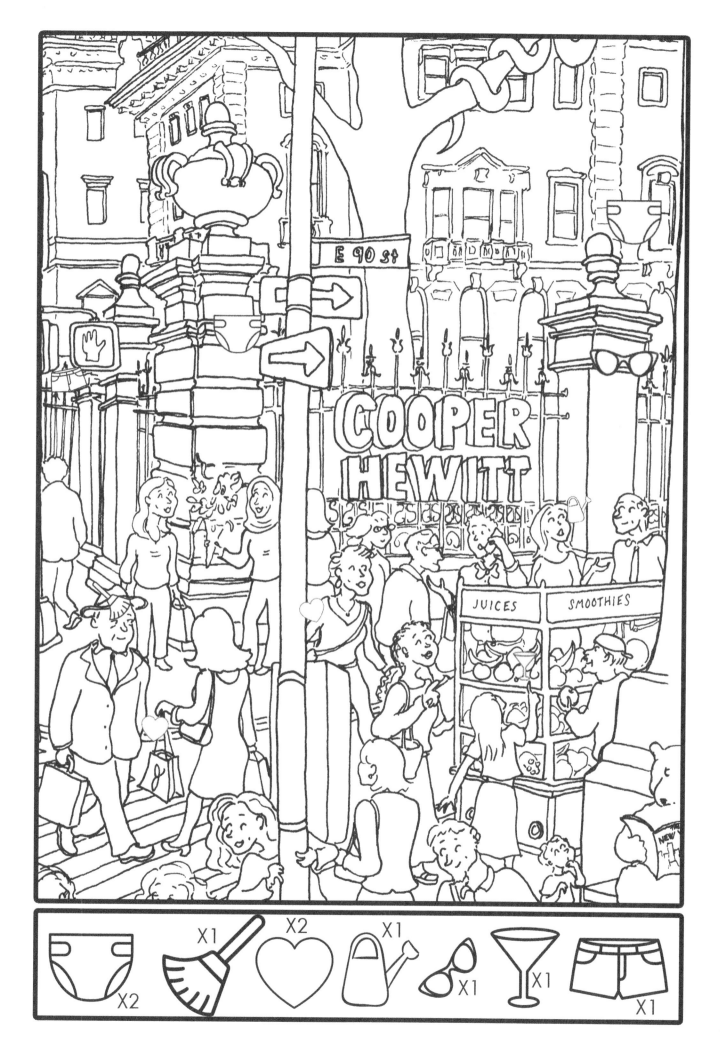

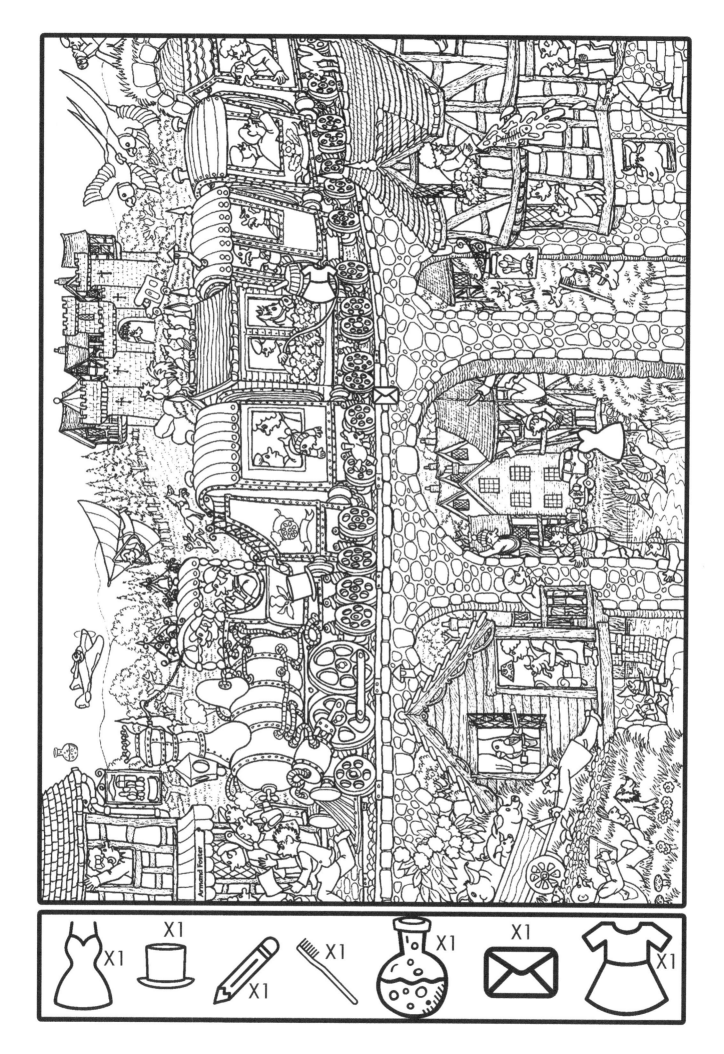

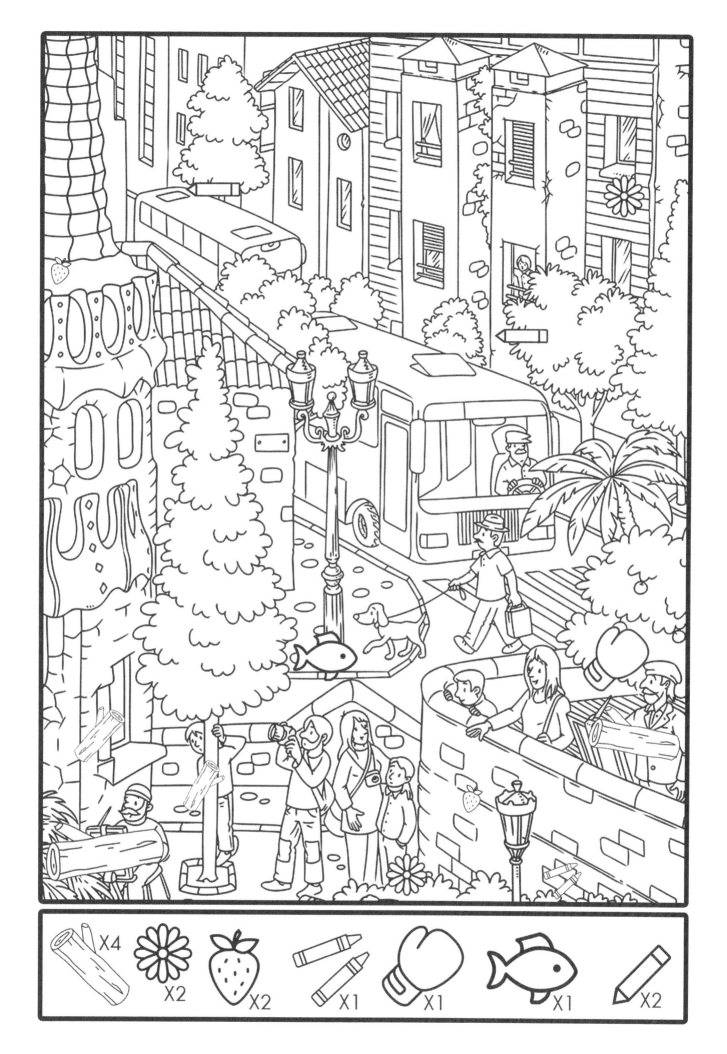

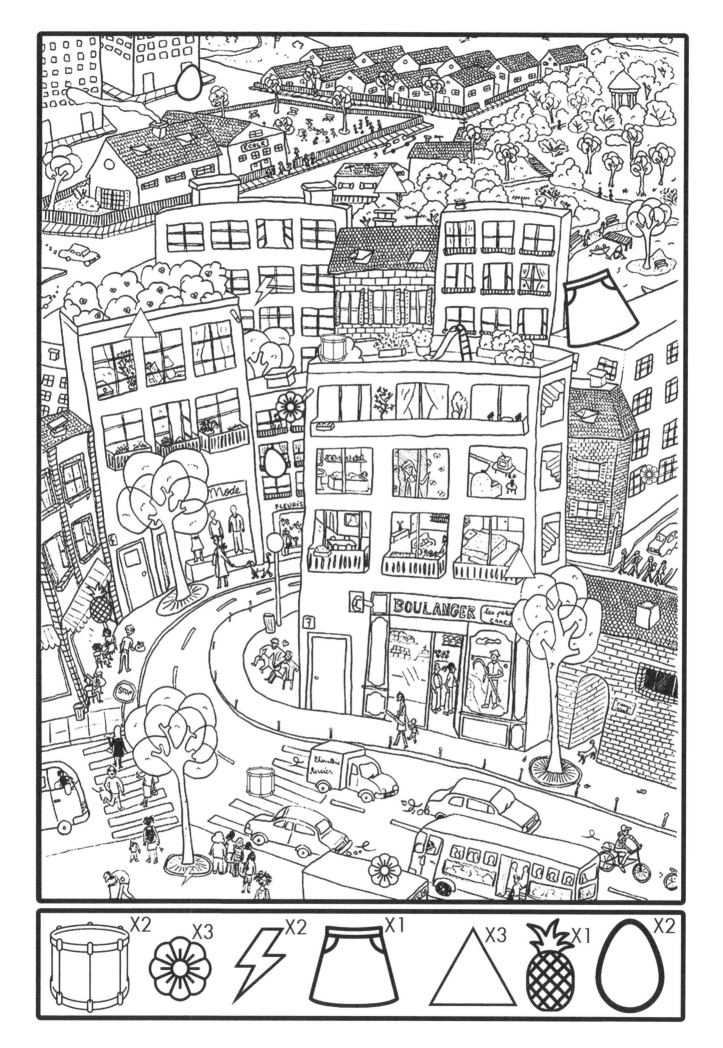

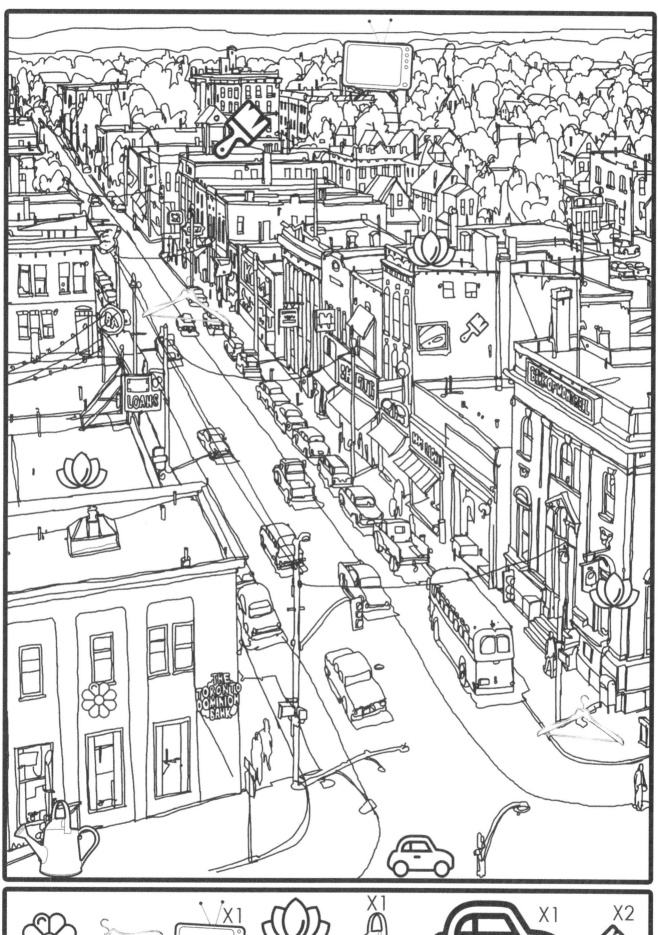
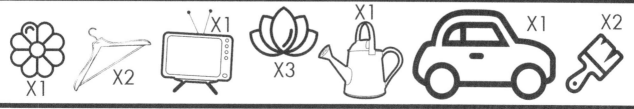

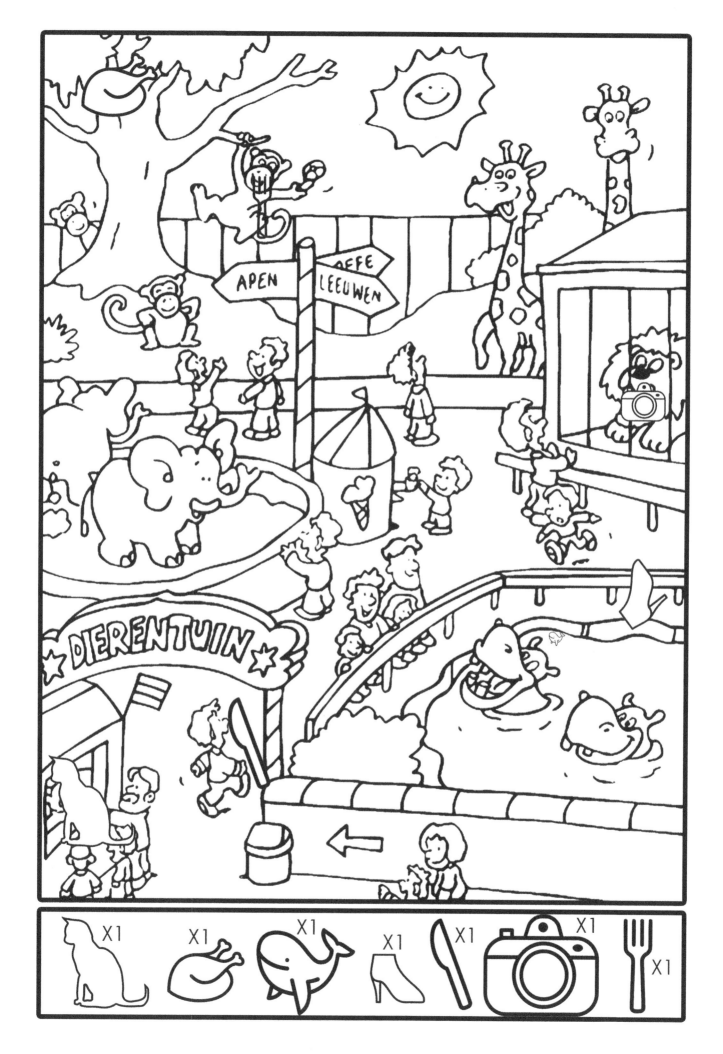

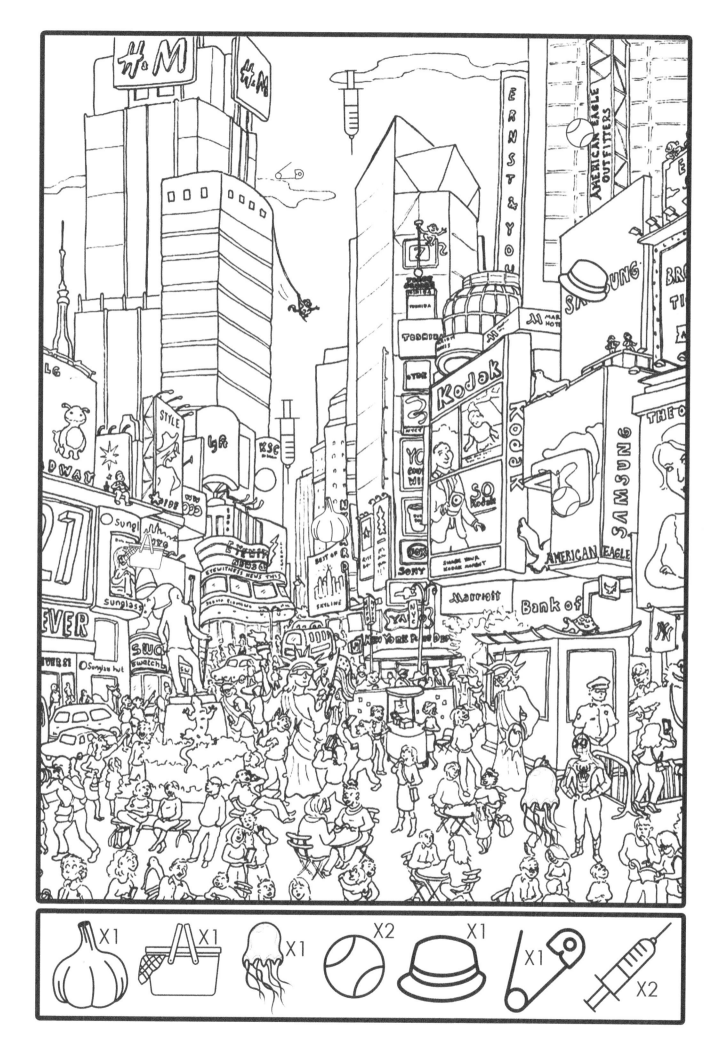

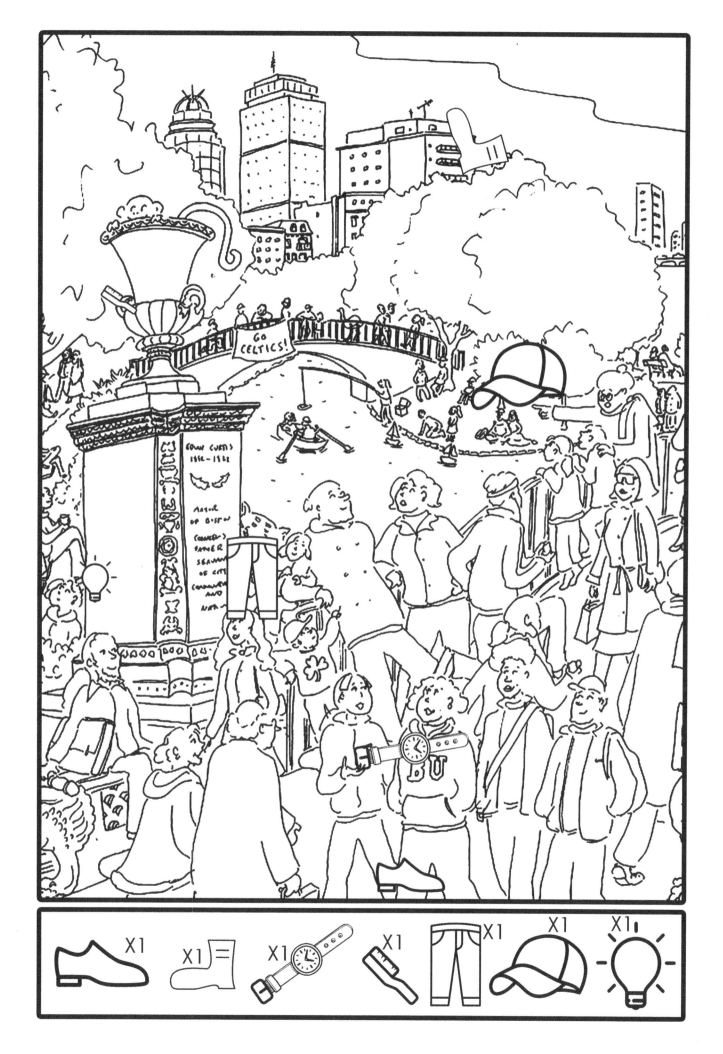

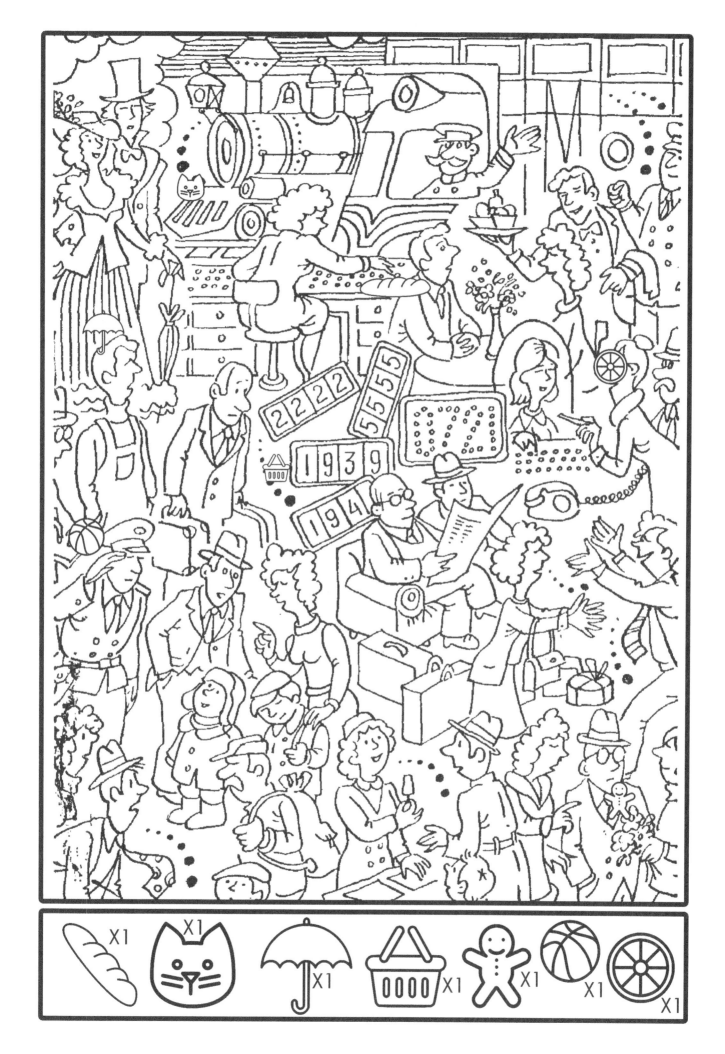

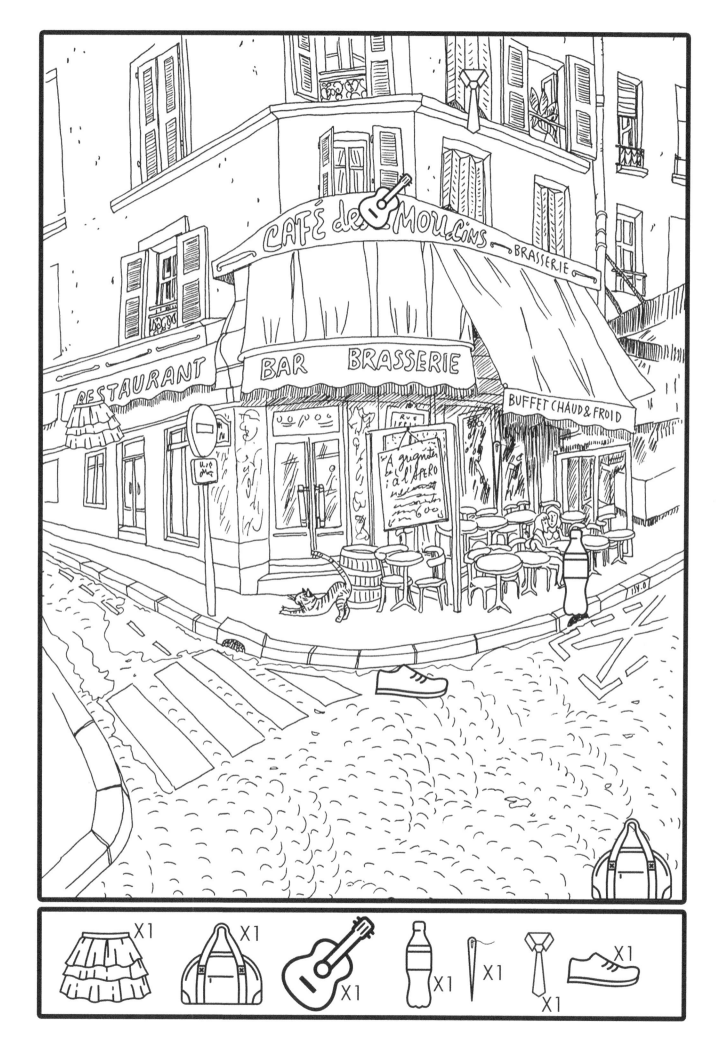

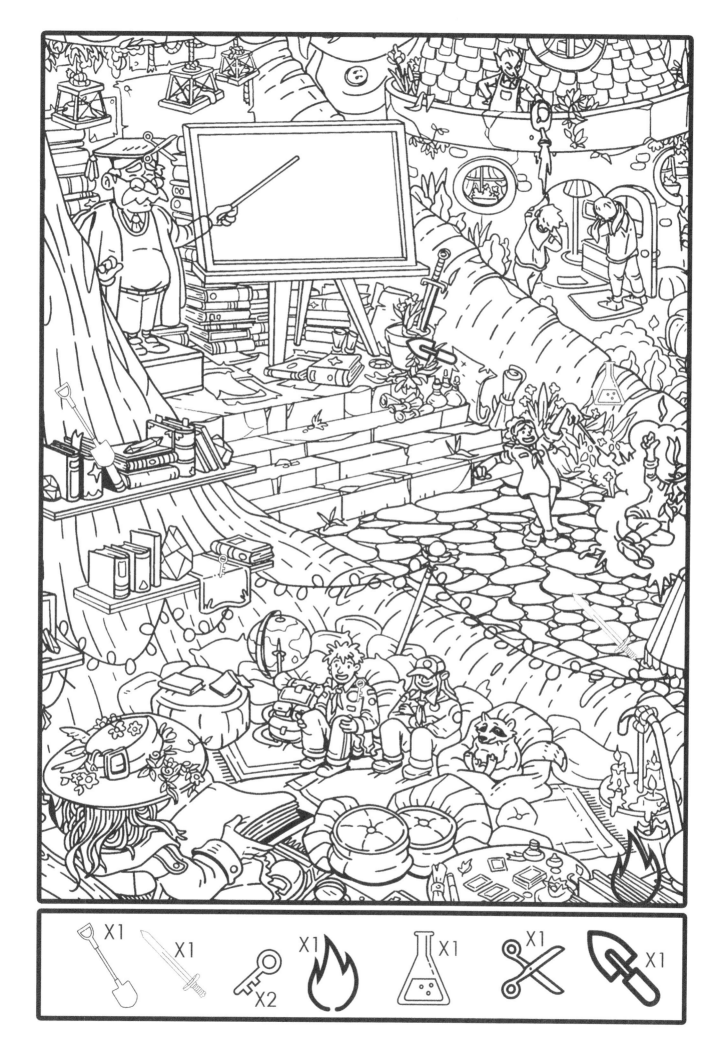

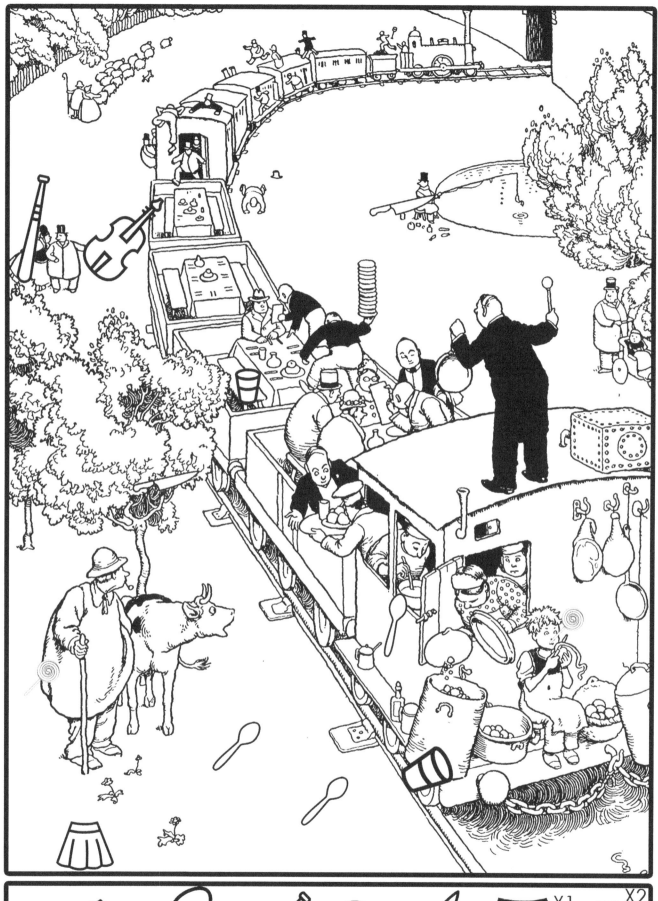
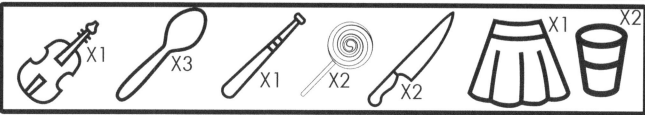

Scan me!
FOR MORE PRODUCT

azbookland.com

THANK YOU FOR BEING
OUR VALUED CUSTOMER
WE WOULD BE GRATEFUL

Made in the USA
Monee, IL
19 December 2024

74688520R00033